AuthorHouse™
1663 Liberty Drive
Bloomington, IN 47403
www.authorhouse.com
Phone: 1 (800) 839-8640

Published by AuthorHouse 5/18/2016

ISBN: 978-1-5246-0933-7 (hc)
978-1-5246-0932-0 (e)

Library of Congress Control Number: 2016908078

Print information available on the last page.

authorHOUSE®

Freddie, the Frog

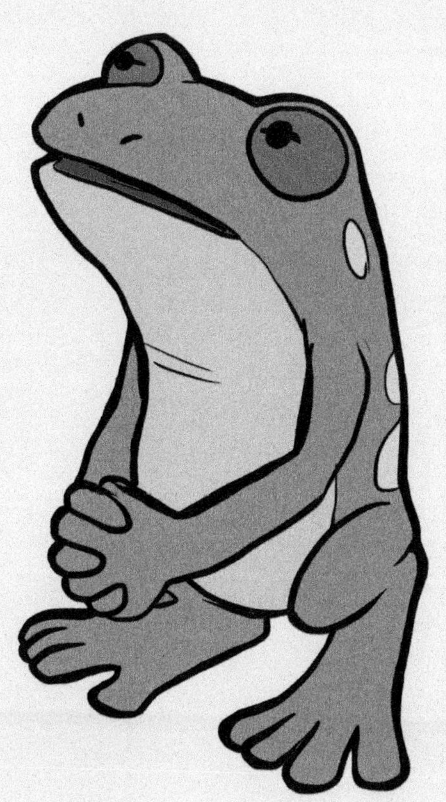

Rena Lotz

For all the little children of this world

When I was just a little frog,

I couldn't jump the smallest log.

My legs were short, not fully grown,

A beautiful lakeside was my home.

The lake had logs and lily pad flowers,

And some older frogs called me a coward.

So I talked to my dad, who
was four times my size,

He said, son, the secret about
jumps lies in your thighs.

I ate more mosquitoes and other flying bugs.

But I never ate a ladybug.

I practiced jumping and found my technique,

Some frogs even said my jumps were unique.

I got bigger and bolder.

My jumps became better as the ones
of the frogs who were older.

ANNUAL
JUMP
COMPETITION!

Then came the spring and as was the tradition,

With the spring came the "Annual
Jump Competition."

I stood in line and waited my turn,

I concentrated on what I had learned.

As the crowd cheered me on,

I pulled my back legs real tight,

Took a deep breath and lunged
forward with might.

JUMPING CH

My jump was the farthest the
town had ever seen,

And my dad was proud when they
crowned me Champeen!

CPSIA information can be obtained
at www.ICGtesting.com
Printed in the USA
BVOW07*0246280516
449846BV00007B/19/P

9 781524 609337